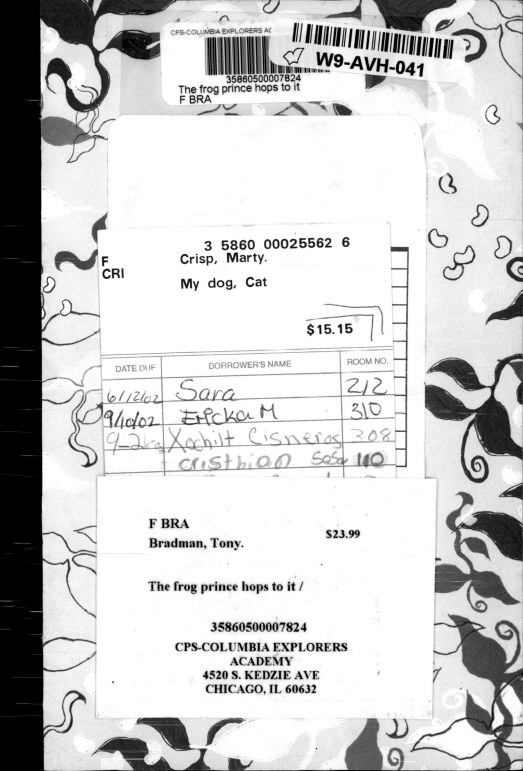

3 5860 00025562 6

F
CRI

Crisp, Marty.

My dog, Cat

$15.15

DATE DUE	BORROWER'S NAME	ROOM NO.
6/12/02	Sara	212
9/10/02	Ericka M	310
9-26-0	Xochilt Cisneros	308
	cristhian sosa	110

AFTER

HAPPILY EVER AFTER

The Frog Prince Hops to It

First published in the United States in 2009
by Stone Arch Books
151 Good Counsel Drive, P.O. Box 669
Mankato, Minnesota 56002
www.stonearchbooks.com

First published by Orchard Books, a division of Hachette Children's Books.
338 Euston Road, London NW1 3BH, United Kingdom

Library of Congress Cataloging-in-Publication Data
Bradman, Tony.
    The Frog Prince Hops to It / by Tony Bradman; illustrated by
Sarah Warburton.
       p. cm. — (After Happily Ever After)
    ISBN 978-1-4342-1303-7 (library binding)
    [1. Ponds—Fiction.] I. Warburton, Sarah, ill. II. Title.
PZ7.B7275Fr 2009
[Fic]—dc22   2008031830

Summary: Prince Freddy is no longer a frog, but he misses the big pond.
However, Princess Daisy thinks the pond is muddy, smelly, and gross. Prince
Freddy must make his wife understand how amazing the pond is before it's
too late.

Creative Director: Heather Kindseth
Graphic Designer: Emily Harris

1 2 3 4 5 6 14 13 12 11 10 09

Printed in the United States of America

AFTER

HAPPILY EVER AFTER

The Frog Prince Hops to It

by Tony Bradman
illustrated by Sarah Warburton

STONE ARCH BOOKS
www.stonearchbooks.com

So Freddy turned back into a
prince, married Daisy,
and lived happily ever after.
And then ...

Prince Freddy quietly opened the
back door of the royal mansion and
slipped inside. He tiptoed down a hall.

He stopped at a door to make sure
there was no one around.

Then he dashed across the hall.

"Whew, I made it!" he thought as he
began to climb the stairs. But suddenly
a shadow fell across him.

He looked up and gulped. His lovely wife, Princess Daisy, was scowling down at him from the landing.

"So you finally came home," she said.

"Listen, darling," said Prince Freddy. "I can explain, honest."

"Don't bother," Daisy said. "I know where you've been. You're covered in mud and you smell gross. When are you going to realize that you're not a frog any more, Freddy?"

Freddy sighed. He had been a frog for a long time. Actually, he had been a prince who had been transformed into a frog by the Wicked Witch.

He had lived at the big pond, but then he met Daisy at a local well.

Eventually she had freed him from the curse with a kiss, and they were married. At first they had been blissfully happy.

But now it seemed they didn't really have much in common. Daisy had become interested in doing charity work, and she was always busy.

She was always getting involved in campaigns for good causes, such as the Fading Fairy Fund, the Hansel and Gretel Kids In Trouble Helpline, even the Keep the Forest Clean and Green Club.

Freddy wasn't exactly sure what he liked doing now he was a person again. He had really enjoyed being a frog, and he missed it. He missed the pond and his froggy friends too.

"I know I'm not a frog any more," Freddy said. "I just like spending time down at the big pond, that's all. What's wrong with that?"

"Nothing, I suppose," Daisy said.
"Not if you think hanging round a
smelly old pond is a good idea. But I
don't. I think it's silly. I wish you could
find something more serious to do.
Now if you'll excuse me, I have some
important letters to write."

And with that, Daisy turned on her
heel and stomped off to her office.

Freddy trudged upstairs to their bedroom. He knew that Daisy didn't like him going to the big pond. That was why he kept sneaking there in secret.

But that obviously hadn't worked.
And he hated tricking her. It just didn't
feel right.

Freddy decided to take a bath. As he
relaxed in the water, he wondered what
to do. He loved Daisy, and he thought
she still loved him. But he loved the big
pond too. If only Daisy felt the same
way about it.

He was sure she would if she understood how amazing it was. So why didn't he show her?

"Yes, that's it!" he said, and leaped out of the bath.

He threw on some clothes and sat down at his desk.

Then he glanced at the calendar on the wall. Daisy's birthday was coming up in a few weeks. "Even better!" he thought, and started making plans.

The morning of Daisy's birthday arrived. When she woke up, Freddy gave her a huge birthday card.

Then he led her down to the royal dining room, where there was an enormous pile of presents.

"Are these all for me?" said Daisy.
"You shouldn't have, Freddy."

She gave him a lovely smile, the kind
he hadn't seen for a while.

"Well, aren't you going to open
them?" said Freddy, smiling back.

Daisy picked up a present and quickly ripped off the wrapping paper.

"Oh, it's a book," she said, her smile fading. "About ponds."

"Yes, and it's got some really great pictures in it," Freddy said.

There were more books too, including
Fairy Tale Ponds, *Life On A Lily Pad*, and
Time for Slime.

There were DVDs about ponds, a pond poster, a special Pond-Watcher's Kit, and even a pair of slippers shaped like frogs.

Daisy's smile vanished, and her bottom lip quivered.

"Well," said Freddy, thinking that he might have made a mistake. "I was planning to take you for a lovely picnic at the big pond."

"I don't believe it!" Daisy wailed.
"This is the worst birthday I've ever had.
I'm beginning to wonder why I married
you in the first place. You're going to
have to make your mind up, Freddy!
It's that pond or me!"

Then she burst into tears and ran out.
Freddy followed and tried to talk to her,
but she locked herself in her office and
refused to see him.

That afternoon, Freddy trudged off to say a final goodbye to the big pond. He had made his choice, but he still felt sad.

He stood by the cool green water.
He listened to the insects buzzing and
the soft, plopping sounds as his froggy
friends dived in. Then he heard another
sound, a banging.

A man was putting up a sign nearby.
Freddy read the sign and felt rather
uneasy.

"Hi," Freddy said. "Would you mind
telling me what that sign means?"

"Sure," said the man. "We're putting an
eight-lane highway through here soon. We
start draining the pond tomorrow."

Freddy was horrified. "You can't do that!" he said. "What's going to happen to all the creatures who live in it?"

"Not my problem," said the man, and walked off. "Goodbye!"

Freddy was angry now. Even if he never went to the big pond again, he just had to save it and his friends! But how? Then it came to him, and he smiled.

He couldn't do it on his own. He
needed a big campaign, and he knew just
the person to help him get it organized.

Freddy ran home as fast as he could.

Soon he was standing outside Daisy's office door again. He raised his hand to knock, but then he stopped.

What if Daisy didn't want to be involved?

But somehow Freddy had a feeling that she would, as long as he could persuade her to talk to him. Soon, she opened her door as soon as she heard him say the words "good cause."

"An eight-lane highway!" she said, just as upset as Freddy. "Of course I'll help. It might only be a smelly old pond, but destroying it would be a total disaster for the forest!"

"Now let me see. We'll have to make some posters, put together a petition, and organize a demonstration," she said. And that was how the 'Save The Big Pond' campaign was born.

Daisy threw herself into it with all her energy. She read the books Freddy had given her and was amazed at how many different types of frogs there were.

"That would be useful for the posters," she thought.

She watched the DVDs too, and they gave her the idea for Wet Rock: The Concert To Save The Big Pond.

She even went to the big pond with
Freddy, where her special pondwatcher's kit
came in very useful. (Although she never
did wear the slippers shaped like frogs.)

The campaign was a huge success,
and the big pond was saved forever.
Freddy was delighted, but he also realized
that he had really loved working on it. So
he asked Daisy if he could help with her
other good causes too.

He took everything very seriously,
and worked just as hard as Daisy. They
became a terrific, unbeatable team.
(Although they made sure they always
had plenty of fun as well.)

So Daisy and Freddy and their froggy
friends really did live **HAPPILY EVER AFTER**.

THE END

ABOUT THE AUTHOR

Tony Bradman writes for children of all ages.
He is particularly well known for his top-selling
Dilly the Dinosaur series. His other titles include
the Happily Ever After series, The Orchard Book
of Heroes and Villains, and The Orchard Book of
Swords, Sorcerers, and Superheroes. Tony lives in
South East London.

ABOUT THE ILLUSTRATOR

Sarah Warburton is a rising star in children's
books. She is the illustrator of the Rumblewick
series, which has been very well received at an
international level. The series spans across both
picture books and fiction. She has also illustrated
nonfiction titles and the Happily Ever After series.
She lives in Bristol, England, with her young baby
and husband.

GLOSSARY

campaign (kam-PAYN)—a series of activities planned to bring about a certain result

corridor (KOR-uh-dur)—hallway

demonstration (DEM-uhn-stray-shun)—a public meeting to show feelings on a topic

disaster (duh-ZASS-tur)—an event that causes much suffering or loss

obviously (OB-vee-uhss-lee)—clearly seen or understood

persuade (pur-SWADE)—to get someone to believe or do something by pleading or giving reasons

petition (puh-TISH-uhn)—a request made in writing to someone who is in charge

royal (ROI-uhl)—related to a king or queen

transformed (transs-FORMED)—to change completely

DISCUSSION QUESTIONS

1. How do you think Freddy felt sneaking around to go to the pond? What else could he have done to make Daisy understand?

2. Daisy was disappointed and sad with the birthday gifts Freddy got her. Discuss a time when you felt disappointed.

3. Daisy and Freddy save the pond and help the environment. What do you do that helps the environment?

WRITING PROMPTS

1. When Freddy wanted to relax, he went to the pond. It was his favorite place. Write a paragraph about your favorite place. Describe where it is and what makes it special.

2. What would have happened if Freddy and Daisy didn't save the pond? Rewrite the ending of the story.

3. Daisy and Freddy held a concert to save the pond. Write a paragraph describing the type of fund raiser you would have to save the pond.

Before there was **HAPPILY EVER AFTER,**
there was **ONCE UPON A TIME** ...

GRAPHIC SPIN

Read the **ORIGINAL** fairy tales in **NEW** graphic novel retellings.

INTERNET SITES

Do you want to know more about subjects related to this book? Or are you interested in learning about other topics? Then check out FactHound, a fun, easy way to find Internet sites.

Our investigative staff has already sniffed out great sites for you!

Here's how to use FactHound:

1. Visit *www.facthound.com*

2. Select your grade level.

3. To learn more about subjects related to this book, type in the book's ISBN number: **143421303X**.

4. Click the **Fetch It** button.

FactHound will fetch the best Internet sites for you!

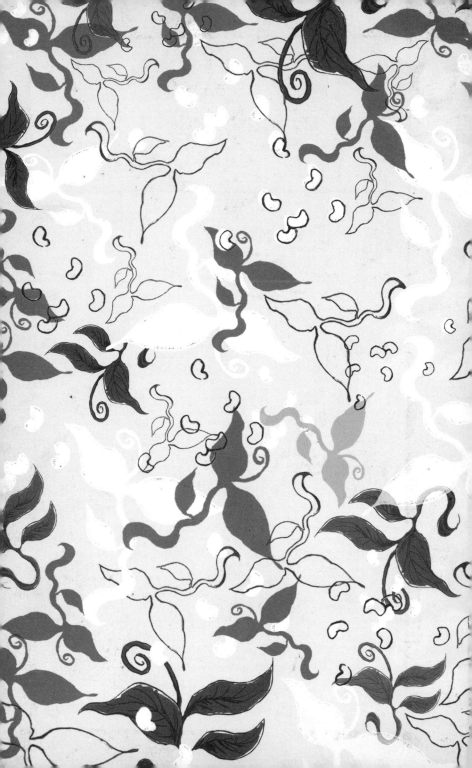